Fenris

Wild Claw Pack, Volume 3

S L Davies

Published by S L Davies, 2023.

FENRIS

First edition. February 1, 2023.

Copyright © 2023 S L Davies.

ISBN: 979-8215140840

Written by S L Davies.

Prologue

E stesius
"Baby," Boyd called as he came into the house on our pack lands. I glanced up at him and smiled.

"What's up?"

"I've just had a call from Connell from the Wild Claw Pack. They have asked if we would be willing to go to their pack lands to help in this war."

I nodded my head. The war against Ettore, the Nephilim, was well known. Boyd was the head alpha, along with his brother, Craig. They had been in contact with the other wolf packs and had agreed that we would all go to the Wild Claw Pack's land and fight alongside them if needed.

"Are they ready for us?" I asked.

Boyd nodded his head. "Yeah, Craig is letting the pack know. Those who want to fight will come with us, but the rest will stay here. We are leaving the elders and the children here too."

I nodded my head. I was glad that Craig and Boyd weren't expecting everyone to fight. This was going to be a bloody battle, and I didn't like the idea that people who were frail or too young would be slaughtered.

"So, who is coming?" I asked.

"We will know once Craig gets here, but I wanted to see if you would be joining us. I'd prefer it if you didn't, but I learned long ago that I wouldn't win if you wanted something."

I snorted. When we first mated twenty years ago, Boyd got a swift crash course because I wasn't about to lie down and have him demand what happens in my life. I was an independent woman, and I would do what I wanted. I didn't know if it was because I was a Pegasus or how I was raised.

"I will come. There will be a need for healers."

Boyd nodded. "That's what I thought you would say," he said with a wry smile as the front door opened and closed, and Craig entered the room. Craig and Boyd were identical twins. It took most people forever to be able to tell the two apart. I'd been able to tell them apart immediately, but that was only because I was mated to Boyd. I imagined that it would be difficult in any other sense.

"All right, I've got the list. We've got fourteen names," Craig said.

"Great, who is coming?"

"Malko, Reece, Jadiel, Luca, Peter, Haiden, Danni, Zoe, Caitlin, Aleigha, Paul, Robin, Steff, and Kason."

There was a mix of people, but the one thing they all had in common was that they were all alphas.

Boyd hummed. "That's a good mix, and it leaves plenty here to protect our members not fighting."

Craig nodded his head. "Some said they might like to come and support us if needed, but they preferred to stay here with their children."

Boyd shook his head. "No. I don't want to take any parents. Only unmated alphas and omegas."

"That's what I said. Three omegas asked if they wanted us to come."

"Who?"

"Terrell, Audriana, and Brice."

Boyd twisted his lips and frowned. "I don't know. They are all young."

"That's why I said I would discuss it with you first."

Terrell was fifteen, and Audriana and Brice were both seventeen. We'd heard about this war for years, and I knew the kids had all grown up knowing about it, so they were eager. However, I was uncomfortable taking kids. I wasn't sure that taking them would be a good idea.

Boyd scrubbed his hand up over his face. "Look, yeah, all right, tell them they can come, but if it looks like it is going to be too dangerous for them, we will send them back."

Craig smiled and nodded his head. "You know they will be fine."

"I know, but I fucking hate this."

"I know you do," Craig answered. "This is a shit situation; the sooner it is over, the better."

Chapter One

Fenris

The pack lands were a hive of activity as we made room for the extra members of the Wild Fang, Silver Bite, and Whitetail Packs. We were still waiting for the Palecrest Pack to arrive. But it meant we had about fifty extra adults and children joining us. We'd managed to disperse them throughout the pack lands. Selene and Canea had helped by building the houses. If only we could make housing as they did. One thought, and they were all built.

After everyone had settled in, the training began. We didn't have much time before this war would commence, so it was essential to get moving on our training. I wanted all the wolves to be at the top of their game. The last thing I wanted was to lose more of our members. I didn't care if they were Wild Claw or from another pack; that pain was still severe.

I was standing in the open field in the center of the pack lands. The sun was warm, and I knew the kids standing around would be hot and bothered by the end of the training, but for now, they were excited to be included. At one end, I'd set up large body bag weights. Each bag weighed the same as an average male.

"Okay," I called, drawing the pup's attention. "What we will be working on today is shifting on the run. When we are at war, there will be times when it will be better for you to fight as a wolf. I want to ensure you can do that on the run."

The pups all watched me eagerly. "Normally, when you would shift, you would first remove your clothes and think about your wolf, calling him or her forward, but when you are on the run, you have to do it all very quickly and in a matter of moments," Herrick said. "This isn't an easy feat, so don't be upset if you struggle. This is why we are practicing."

I smiled at Herrick. He had the patience of a saint. He was a fantastic Papa and grandfather to Sable's kids. And the kids, strangers or not, all seemed to gravitate toward him.

"For this task, I want you to start by running toward the bags; when Herrick or I yell now, I want you to call your wolf forward and continue to run toward the bag."

The kids all looked worried; I could tell they wanted to get it right. However, I knew how difficult this was. It took practice and time. The time that this war, unfortunately, wasn't going to grant us, so we would have to push the kids a little more than what they would typically do.

The other pack leaders stood around the field watching.

"Ready?" Herrick called.

All the kids nodded their heads. "Okay, start running," I called and watched as they took off toward the bags. Once they were only meters from the bag, I roared. "Now."

There wasn't one of the kids that managed to shift on the run; they all had to come to a complete halt before they could shift, making me chuckle. It was what I had expected to happen. All of the pups came running back in their shifted forms. Little wolves sat down in front of me.

"Okay, shift back, pups," I instructed. The kids altered, and I looked at each of them. "That was tricky, huh?"

"Yeah, I don't know how to run and shift; it is like I can't do both things at once," one of the pups, Zachary, said.

I nodded my head. "I understand that. It isn't an easy task, and normally you guys would get to learn it at your own pace; we wouldn't be hurrying you. However, because of this war, we want to ensure you can run if needed."

"Do you think Ettore will try to kill us?" another boy from the Silver Bite Pack, Ryan asked.

I sighed and sat down on the ground in front of the kids. Herrick handed out blankets to wrap around their naked bodies and sat beside me. The leaders of the other packs came and sat beside us, having obviously heard Ryan's question.

"I'd like to hope he wouldn't, but honestly, I don't know, Ryan," I answered truthfully.

Ryan's eyes welled with tears. "I don't want to die."

"Oh mate, come here," I said as I pulled the boy, that couldn't have been older than six, into my lap. I kissed the top of his fair hair and looked down at him.

"I don't want you to die either, and that is why we are working so hard on this training. All of you need to be able to not only fight but to run away. I would prefer you all to run away if danger came here."

"You don't want us to fight?" Zachary asked. He was the son of the Whitetail pack leader Tasha and her mate, Will.

"No, I don't. I don't really want anyone to fight. But I recognize that for some, that is not a choice we have. Ettore's army is large, and we will need members to battle him. However, you are all the next generation; once we return to the creator, to the After World, it will be your job to take over as pack leaders and pack members. That is why I'd rather you all run if you had the chance."

Zachary nodded his head and glanced over at his Mama, that was sitting to my right. "Do you think like that too, Mama?"

Tasha nodded her head. "I do. I want my children to be safe. And if that means for you to run, then that is what I'd like you to do."

Zachary nodded again and sighed. "I guess we better learn how to shift on the run."

I smiled. "You all ready to get back to it?"

The kids all nodded, and we stood. "This time, I'm going to use my alpha tone to help you shift so that you get the feeling of what you are doing as you are running," Herrick said.

The kids lined up after dropping their blankets. At least now that they were all naked, it would be easier for them to shift without the concern of tearing out their clothes.

"Ready? Start running," I instructed. The kids all took off toward the bags at the end of the field.

They were only meters away when Herrick roared. "Shift," his alpha tone rippled through the air as it hit each kid. I watched them alter mid-stride. Now we just had to teach them to be able to do it on their own.

Chapter Two

B oyd
    "We are all set," I said to Estesius as I wrapped my arm around her shoulders and kissed her cheek. She looked up at me with that slight smile she always gave me from the first moment I met her.

It was hard to believe that we had been together for almost twenty years. I still remembered the first day I ever met her. Craig and I were at an arcade; we were pains in the ass like always and competing against each other on pinball machines. Craig and I were as tight as possible, but we were each other's biggest rivals.

I was cackling as I kicked Craig's ass on the pinball machine when Estesius's scent wrapped around me. I gasped and spun, catching the eye of the most beautiful woman I'd ever seen. She was staring at me with wide eyes. Her hair was a mix of blonde, purple and pink at the time. She had the most gorgeous purple eyes I'd ever seen, and I couldn't have stopped my feet from gravitating toward her if I had tried.

In the middle of the arcade, I took her hand and leaned down to kiss her. I received a slap in the face which quickly snapped me out of it.

"You ask a lady before you manhandle her," Estesius snapped at me.

"Man, what the fuck?" Craig had asked.

I apologized like crazy and quickly explained that Estesius was my mate. The rest was history, Estesius had agreed to go home with me, and she never left. As it turned out, Pegasus was as affected by me as her. The only difference was that she had more control—something I've loved about her ever since.

"Great," Estesius said. "Was Petra okay about stepping into the head alpha role while you and Craig left?"

Petra was our sister and the next alpha in the pack line. She was mated to our best friend that we grew up with, Bryan. The two of them had eight children. I swear that woman was constantly pregnant. Something that Estesius and I hadn't been successful in. We'd seen doctors, but as it turned out unless we found our other mate, there would be no baby for us. The day that we found that out was hard. Not only did I have to get used to the thought that I would have to share my mate, but that somewhere out there was another person who was key to unlocking our family. We didn't know where they were or who they were; we just had to hope that Mother fate blessed us by bringing them to us.

"Yeah, she is happy to do it. Happy is probably the wrong word; she'd growled at Craig and me and said something about not having enough on her fucking plate," I said with a chuckle.

Estesius laughed. "I can envision that. But running the pack isn't as stressful as raising her brood."

I grinned and nodded my head, kissing the side of Estesius's head again. "Ready to start heading off to Lalbert?"

Estesius glanced around the living room. Most of our furniture was still in place; we'd decided only to take our personal belongings, paperwork, clothes, that sort of thing. We were walking into this war; there were bound to be casualties, even with the gods on our side. After this war, I had full intention of coming home. Of course, if I was still alive to go home. I couldn't think like that. The thought that we might not all be alive at the end of it was terrifying, but one that was a reality.

The front door swung open, and Craig stepped into the living room with his mate, Raleigh, behind him. She had decided that she would come along with his three sons. I knew that Craig wasn't happy about it. Hell, I wasn't happy about it. But the one thing the Palecrest Pack had was strong-willed women. We wouldn't love and respect them if they weren't strong women, but it made moments like this difficult.

Tommy and Nevin, Craig's sons, came into the living room behind their parents. The boys were identical twins also. Both were sixteen, tall and dark-haired, just like Craig. Looking at the four of us together, you'd swear we were all brothers.

"Everyone is ready; we are just waiting on you two before we get on the road," Craig said.

I breathed in deeply and nodded my head. I'd be lying if I said I wasn't nervous about this. We'd known about the coming war for years. It was something we'd been told about by our parents. But it was one of those events we thought were way off in the future that we wouldn't see. Then, when Connell from the Wild Claw Pack contacted me a month ago, I knew that this wouldn't be a war we could avoid.

I never broke a promise to my Papa. I'd promised Papa before he died that Craig and I would lend our assistance when the war came. So, we were packed and ready to go to Lalbert and fight a battle to protect the supernatural race.

I nodded my head and linked my fingers with my mates. "Let's go."

Craig nodded and turned to walk out of the house. I followed him out with Estesius by my side. Glancing back at home, I sent a little prayer into the universe. Even if I couldn't come back, I hoped that Estesius would.

Chapter Three

Fenris

"That's it, Ryan," I called as I watched the pup swing and kick at one of the older boys, Traison. We'd spent the morning sparring and teaching the smaller ones how to get out of holds. It wouldn't help if they came up against magic, but I felt it was just as vital for them to learn how to fight with their fists and weapons and use their magic.

Everything and everyone had been moving at warp speed. From the news we were getting back, Ettore was assembling his troops, and there was a rumor that he was going to come to the Devil's Advocates compounds in an attempt to fight us there. He didn't realize that the gods had warded down the place that he would never be able to step foot on.

I was worried about what would happen when he worked it out. An average person would give up their idea of world domination. An average person would realize that their fight was already lost. But Ettore was far from average. He was as crazy as a hatter, and that scared me. I couldn't predict what he was going to do next.

Everyone was working hard at trying to gather as much intel as possible. Some Wild Claw members could use their powers to get into the training center. But we had to be so careful. If Ettore discovered them, they would be instantly executed. I didn't want to lose anyone. It was a silly thought; I knew there would be wartime deaths. I just hated the idea of it.

When we lost Mondo in the facility explosions, it rocked everyone. Samara, his mate, wasn't coping all these months. The gods had agreed to send her to Middle Earth to stay protected, but her pain was overwhelming. I worried about her. I didn't think she would ever be the same. Mondo was not just her fated mate; he was the love of her life. Her whole world revolved around that man.

"They are doing really well," Selene said as she came to stand beside me. It was still taking a lot for me to get used to the goddess we worshipped, walking around and talking to us as if she wasn't a goddess.

I nodded my head. "They are. Although I don't want the kids to fight, I know they should be able to run and protect themselves if trouble comes."

Selene looked over at me and smiled. "That's what we can hope for."

"Have we got any more word on Ettore?"

"He is growing crazier by the day. With every power he takes on as his own, his mind shatters a little more."

"Do you think that will kill him?"

Selene shrugged her shoulders. "Anyone else, and I would say so, but this is the prophecy; if he were to die without this war coming to fruition, then the prophecy wouldn't happen, and that could mean devastating events for all of our worlds."

I nodded my head. That was one thing that the gods and goddesses talked a lot about. Making one little change can alter the path of something else. It was why the gods didn't just step in and kill Ettore. I understood it, but I was not too fond of it. I hated that this war had to happen. I hated that this was the only way to create a new world where supernaturals, gods, goddesses, and humans could be at peace.

"All right, kids, let's wrap it up for today and come into a huddle," I called. The kids all stopped sparring and came running to stand in a circle around me. Selene passed out water bottles to each of them. Once they'd had their drink and were ready, I spoke again. "You all did very well today; I'm proud of your progress. It won't be long, and you will be ready to start working with weapons."

Tyson cheered and rubbed his hands together, making me laugh. That boy would cheer just about anything. He loved all of the training and was the last one to stop. If he were human, he would probably be diagnosed with ADHD or something similar, but as a wolf, it was just him. He was an alpha and the son of the Wild Fang head alpha, Jay.

"That's it for today; head over to the rec room; I believe there is a big banquet waiting for you all."

"A banquet?" Ryan asked with wide eyes. That boy thought more with his belly than any of the others.

I chuckled and nodded my head. "Yes. A banquet. It is Iver's seventeenth birthday today, and he has invited you all to join him for a party."

The kids all cheered and ran toward the large hall we used as a dining room to feed everyone. The Devil's Advocates, Onyx Rebels, and many others were all expected to join us for the party. Any birthday was celebrated, but in recent times it was something that we didn't put as much stock on with this war taking precedence. Iver's birthday was the perfect excuse to let our hair down and relax.

"I will go, but Fenris, just stand here a moment," Selene said as she started to walk away.

"What?" I asked as I turned to face her in time to see Ward coming toward me with another man.

"Hey, Fenris, this is Boyd, one of the head alphas from the Palecrest Pack," Ward introduced.

My eyes widened, and my mouth dropped open as Boyd's scent hit me like a brick. I was floored. How could this be? My mate.

"Fucking hell," Boyd groaned as he walked straight toward me. Without hesitation, he pulled me into his arms and pressed his lips against mine.

I groaned and thrust my hips against him, feeling his hardened length press into my thigh. My tongue tangled with Boyd's, and I thrust my hands into his hair. Boyd's hands roamed down over my back to my ass, pulling me tighter against him. His scent was everywhere, and I could only think about how I wanted him. I wanted to see his ass spread wide as my cock speared inside him.

"Um, guys," Ward said, breaking the spell that had fallen over us.

When we broke the kiss, I turned to Ward, who was laughing so hard he had tears running down his face.

"Well, I guess you guys are fated, but here on the field probably isn't the best place to mate."

"Holy shit," I said, shaking my head. "Yeah, sorry."

Boyd's cheeks tinted pink. "Sorry. I got carried away; it happened when I met Estesius too."

"Estesius?"

"My mate. Well, I guess our mate. She's a Pegasus; um, she is in the dining hall with the kids. Shit, this is weird," Boyd mumbled as he rubbed the back of his neck.

"Is Estesius an omega?"

Boyd nodded his head. "Yeah. We always knew there was another person out there for us. Pegasus don't get pregnant unless they have all their mates, so we knew there was someone. I didn't mean to paw you the minute I met you."

I chuckled and shrugged my shoulders. "I don't mind the pawing. But I would like to meet Estesius."

Boyd grinned and nodded his head. "She is probably going to be as shocked as I am. Oh, and word of warning, don't do to her what I just did to you; she will snot you one." Boyd rubbed over his cheek as if remembering when he first met his mate.

I snorted and nodded my head. "Noted. Keep my hands to myself until invited."

Ward cackled and slung his arm around my shoulders. "Come on, you two lovers, let's go and get you both mated."

Chapter Four

E stesius

I'd been a little nervous about going to the Wild Claw Pack. Everyone was incredible. Typically wolf shifter packs didn't interact with one another. It wasn't that we didn't like each other or had an issue, but we tended to stick to our own. Not that I was a wolf shifter. But being mated to one made me a stand-in wolf shifter.

"You have all come on a great day," Anghus, the President of the Devil's Advocates, said as we stood in the dining hall. It was a hive of activity.

"So, I heard," I replied with a smile. "I wish I'd known earlier I would have brought a gift for Iver."

Anghus shook his head and waved his hand. "No need for that. The boy gets spoiled enough as it is."

I smiled. The boy in question stood at around six and a half feet and looked more like a man than a boy. He was muscular and looked at everyone with seriousness. Yet when he smiled, his entire face lit up. There was no denying who his father was. They could have been brothers.

"Hello, I haven't had a chance to meet you yet. I'm Joachim, Anghus's mate, and Iver, McKenna and Canea's Papa."

I smiled and stuck my hand out to shake Joachim's. "It's wonderful to meet you. I'm Estesius; I'm mated to Boyd from the Palecrest Pack. You'll meet Boyd soon; Ward took him to the field to meet Fenris."

"Oh, amazing. I love having all the new people around. I hope that once this is all over, we will have a chance to still stay in contact."

I nodded my head. "I think we will. Boyd and Craig have wanted to join our packs for a long time, and I know that the Wild Claw Pack and Devil's Advocates are very close."

Anghus nodded. "Yeah, we are more like siblings now. Although we run independently, we are pretty much one big group."

"I like that."

Iver looked up from where he was signing with his fingers to another man and came over to us. "Hey there, you are Estesius."

I smiled. "I am. And you are the cthulu I've heard so much about."

Iver grinned and nodded his head. "I'm not sure how I feel about being so infamous."

I laughed. "At least you are known for the good things that will happen."

Iver breathed in deeply and nodded his head. "I like to hope so."

Suddenly a scent wrapped around me, and my eyes widened as I gasped. I spun on my heel and looked toward the door where Ward, Boyd, and another beautiful man were coming. His dark hair was twisted into tight braids over his head. His skin was chocolate, and his brown eyes bore into mine.

"My mate," I whispered.

As I walked toward Boyd and the other man, my feet seemed to have a mind of their own. Ward was grinning like a loon as I approached them.

"Estesius, he's our mate," Boyd said.

I looked over at Boyd and smiled. "He is," I agreed before turning back to the beautiful man. "What is your name?"

"Fenris," he answered. His voice was deep and velvety. I groaned and pressed my thighs together. I wondered if this man's voice could make me cum alone.

"I think we should go find somewhere a little more private," Boyd suggested.

I nodded my head. He was right; I couldn't hold my heat off for long. This was different. When I first met Boyd, I was on heat suppressants, but I'd stopped them years ago when Boyd and I mated. I could feel my skin tightening, and I was feeling hot all over.

"We can go to my home if that suits you?" Fenris asked.

I nodded my head. "That would be great."

Boyd slipped his fingers between mine as we followed Fenris from the dining hall and down the dirt path toward the homes dotted across the yard. We walked in silence, but everything seemed to be heightened. The colors, the scents, and the sounds all around us. My skin was starting to itch, and my heat was setting in and coming in quickly.

The crunch of our feet on the dirt road set my nerves on fire. "We need to hurry," I grunted out.

Boyd looked down at me and nodded his head. "She is going into heat."

Fenris looked over his shoulder and took my hand in his. "In here," he said as we walked toward a house and through the front door. I was pressed hard against Boyd. No sooner had the door shut than my body rubbed all over him.

Boyd groaned. "Oh baby," he moaned as he kissed me firmly and tangled his tongue with mine.

I wanted these men, and I wanted them now.

Chapter Five

B oyd
  Estesius's arousal filled the air; it was the hottest thing I could ever smell. The scent was all her, but then add to that the smell of her dripping wet pussy, and I was in heaven. It was strange, I'd never been with a guy before, but fuck did I want Fenris to be fucking me into the mattress.

My tongue wrestled with Estesius's as my hands tore at her clothes, shredding them into rags. As soon as she was naked, I turned Estesius to face Fenris, who was watching us. My mate's eyes were glazed, and she was in full heat. There would be no time to stop and get to know Fenris. She needed to mate, and she needed it immediately.

"Isn't she beautiful?" I purred and watched Fenris's eyes flare with heat as he gazed over her naked body.

"So beautiful," he groaned. Having been with Estesius for so long, I knew every part of her body to touch that she loved. I smirked and let my fingers wander down over her sensitive nipples. Her nipples pebbled under my touch, and a small moan fell from her lips.

"Lean back against me, baby; let Fenris see that pretty pussy," I instructed.

Estesius didn't need further instruction as she leaned her body into mine and widened her legs. Fenris licked over his bottom lip, and his eyes narrowed on her dripping cunt.

"Lick her," I directed.

Fenris instantly fell to his knees; his hands grasped Estesius's hips as he mouthed at her mound. Slowly and teasingly, he licked up through her folds, taking his time to taste every little inch of her. Estesius leaned further into me and wound her fingers up through my hair; I kissed and suckled on her neck; I allowed my fangs to lengthen slightly and skimmed them across the sensitive skin below her ear.

"Yes," Estesius hummed. I may have been a wolf shifter, but my and Craig's Mama was a vampire. While Craig didn't have many vampire traits, I had them in spades. It was the only thing that wasn't identical about us. I allowed my fangs to penetrate the skin, just enough to draw blood and fill my mate with pleasure. Estesius grunted and grasped Fenris by the hair as she ground her pussy against his face.

"Right there, god, yes," she cried. Fenris held tighter as he continued to eat my mate, drawing her pleasure higher and higher. Estesius's head was thrown back against my shoulder, and I pinched at her nipples, pulling the orgasm from her body. Her body stiffened with a final shudder and a cry as she soared over the edge of pleasure.

Fenris slowed the pressure on her clit and kissed, sucking her folds into his mouth, licking every bit of honey she poured onto his face. Estesius opened her eyes which had darkened to a deep violet.

"It's time," she said. "Kiss him, Boyd." I nodded and slowly led her over to the couch as I stripped from my clothes. Fenris copied, and together we stood naked.

I smirked at my little vixen and turned my attention to Fenris. Stalking toward him, I reached out and grasped him by the hips. I skimmed my hands down over his chest and abs to his hardened length; it was long and thick, not dissimilar to mine. The only difference where I was white, and he was brown. I stroked my hand gently up and down Fenris's shaft as I pressed my lips against his, tangling our tongues together.

Fenris groaned into my mouth as he took hold of my dick and started to stroke it in time with me. Our moans were heady, and when I glanced over at Estesius, her fingers were buried deep inside her pussy.

"Do you want us to mate before or after we fuck you?" I asked her.

Estesius bit into her bottom lip as she considered the question. "While you fuck me."

I grinned and looked up into Fenris's eyes. "Do you have lube?" he nodded and let go of me; when he returned, he held up a bottle of lube.

I took it from him and opened the cap. "Do you want her ass or her pussy?"

"Fuck," Fenris grunted as he looked over at Estesius. "Which would you rather?"

Estesius hummed. "I know what Boyd feels like in my pussy, so I think you should take that, and Boyd can take my ass."

I nodded my head and spread lube along my shaft. "Fenris lay on the floor. Baby, you straddle him."

I stepped in behind Estesius and kneeled between Fenris's legs. The two of them moved into position. Estesius and Fenris moaned simultaneously as she sunk onto his shaft. I watched as she rocked back and forth, kissing him and stroking her hands over his arms and shoulders.

Pouring more lube on my fingers, I slowly pushed a finger inside Estesius's tight hole before sliding in a second and scissoring them, stretching her open ready for my dick. Estesius moaned as she thrust back against my fingers.

"That feels so good. I want more, Boyd; I want you inside me."

I smiled and nodded. "I'm coming, baby," I assured her.

Once she had managed to take four fingers, I slowly lined the head of my dick up with her back entrance and pushed forward. Estesius and Fenris groaned as my cock rubbed against his through the thin lining between us.

"Oh god, more Boyd, more," Estesius moaned.

I snapped my hips hard, and Estesius let out a long cry. She gripped Fenris's shoulders as I pounded hard into her, feeling my knot grow. My fangs itched with need. My alpha and wolf were screaming at me to take our mate. Fenris must have been thinking the same as I felt his knot lock in place before he leaned forward and sunk his teeth hard into Estesius's shoulder.

Estesius screamed as her body spasmed, clenching hard around my knot and forcing it into her ass. I pushed Estesius down as I leaned over her and bit into Fenris's shoulder. The wolf howled, and I realized that Estesius was marking him simultaneously. I could feel each throb on his dick as he filled our mate with more and more cum.

Fenris growled and leaned forward; his teeth penetrated my shoulder, sending me over the edge. My orgasm washed over me, taking me to heights I'd never been. When we slowly returned to reality, our breathing had evened out, and our knots were firmly lodged inside Estesius.

Estesius let out a little giggle as she looked back at me over my shoulder. "I am going to have to start stretching. I want to feel both your knots in my pussy at once."

Fenris and I groaned, and our cocks throbbed, making Estesius laugh harder. This girl might kill me.

Chapter Six

F enris
"Sore?" Boyd asked as I gingerly sat at the table the following morning. I smirked and nodded my head. My ass was tender, but I wasn't going to complain.

Boyd sat carefully in the seat opposite me, making me chuckle. He snickered and shook his head before taking a sip from his coffee. I didn't think any of us got to sleep last night. We were going to need a strong coffee to get us through today. Unfortunately, life wasn't going to stop for us to fuck as much as we wanted.

"Sorry guys," Connell called as he opened the front door. "Please be decent."

I cackled and looked over at the kitchen doorway as he came in. "We are decent. What's up?"

"Kade asked all the alphas to meet him at the Devil's compound. There was an attack early this morning."

"Shit," I growled. "Do you know any other information?"

Connell shook his head. "Not yet, but I think it was bad; I've never seen Kade so angry."

I winced and nodded. "All right, I'll wake Estesius, and we will meet you there."

"Thank you," Connell replied with a smile. "And congratulations."

I grinned at my brother-in-arms. "Thank you, man."

I walked into the bedroom where Estesius was getting dressed. "I was just coming to wake you."

"I heard," she laughed. "I'd prefer to be in bed still."

"You can stay if you'd rather."

Estesius shook her head. "No, this is part of living in wartime."

I nodded and left the room to wait in the living room. It wasn't long before we left and headed over to the Devil's compound. I rode my bike while Estesius and Boyd drove around. When we reached the main house of the Devil's compound, several members of the Palecrest pack all greeted Boyd and Estesius with hugs and congratulations. One man identical to Boyd came over to me and pulled me into his arms.

"Welcome to the family. I'm Craig."

I smiled as I hugged him back. "Nice to meet you, and thank you. I'm Fenris, and you are also part of the Wild Claw Pack."

Craig grinned and patted me on the back. "Well, we better get inside and find out what has happened."

I nodded and inhaled deeply; for Kade to call us together meant it wouldn't be good. Something had happened, and it was terrible. My stomach twisted as I thought about what Ettore could have done. Looking around as we walked into the large hall of the main house, I noticed that the AJE authority members, Onyx Rebels, and many of the Devils were already inside. I felt relief that the attack didn't appear to be on any of the members who were part of this war. But that filled me with another sense of dread. Who had Ettore attacked?

"Thank you, everyone, for coming," Kade said as we all took our seats. I'd never seen the Nephilim's eyes so dark. They were so red that they were practically glowing. The anger that was pouring from him was almost palpable. "I'm afraid there has been another attack. This one, however, was on humans."

My eyes widened. Ettore had never attacked humans before. I wondered what had changed. From the look on everyone's faces, I could see they were thinking the same thing.

"Humans?" Anghus asked.

Kade sighed and nodded his head. "Hayden Magrath from the homicide unit contacted me because he believed that Ettore carried out the attack. At four this morning, the police got a report of an attack on four houses. The adults in the homes were all killed. The houses all had two adults and at least one child in them. Children ranging from the age of ten to fifteen are missing."

"What is he wanting the children for?" Israel asked.

Kade glanced over at Hades, who stood and walked to stand beside Kade. "We got news today that Ettore has captured an angel."

"He's trying to make a Nephilim," I gasped.

Hades looked over at me and nodded his head.

"How?" Boyd questioned. "Ettore is a Nephilim; how has he got the power to be not only ensnare an angel but a goddess as well?"

"Aphrodite is a demi-god, and the angel, Domiel, is lower in rank. They aren't powerful," Hades answered.

"But they still should be more powerful than Ettore," I replied.

Hades nodded his head. "You are right. We don't know how he has managed to capture them. Aphrodite, he promised her a life of love and mateship, but we don't know how he managed to keep her captive."

I scrubbed my hands up over my face. This was a mess. How the fuck was this Nephilim so powerful that he could capture and hold a goddess. Would it even fucking matter that we had the gods on our side?

"Even if he is trying to breed a Nephilim, human pregnancies take nine months to complete; then the child won't come into their powers until they are three at the earliest. There has to be something else going on; this doesn't make sense," Anghus said.

Hades nodded his head. "I agree with you. I don't understand what is going on. And we are just assuming that he has taken Domiel to procreate with the humans he took this morning."

"Could Domiel be working with him?" Memphis, one of the AJE authority members, asked.

Hades nodded his head. "We have considered that. Odin is in the After World, trying to find out. There should have been no way Ettore got to the After World, but we are running on the back foot here trying to catch up."

"I feel like this is all we have been doing," Anghus growled. "How the fuck do we get in front of this cunt?"

Hades sighed. "I understand your anger. I really do. I want to say to hell with the prophecy and go in and kill him. But that will change the world drastically."

"For the worse?" I asked.

Hades looked over at me and nodded his head. "If I kill Ettore now, there will be drastic consequences. I'm sorry. I know this is shit, and you all feel defeated and are biting at the bit to end it, but there is always a reason."

"And how many innocents are going to die in the process?" Anghus growled. I could feel his anger, and I knew that he was struggling. We all were. It felt like the gods were stalling us.

Hades sighed. "I'm sorry. I really am."

"Do you want him dead?" I asked. "Or are you all working with him in secret?"

Boyd gasped beside me. "Fenris," Connell growled in warning.

I stood from my seat and turned to my best friend. "What? Their idea to go and hit the breeding facilities at once got Mondo killed. A young girl from the Devil's Advocates was killed. How many more of us are they going to send to slaughter? They can shut this cunt down, and we are constantly told it's not time. When is the time? When will we finally say enough is enough and do something?"

"I understand your anger, Fenris," Odin said as he stepped into the room. "I'm sorry that it feels like we are working against you. I assure you that we are not. I understand your impatience and agree that losing members of your pack and families feels unfair. However, I assure you that we are working with you. There is a reason for every action that we make. This war will affect not just the earth but Middle Earth and the After World. We need to have things in place to ensure we win this."

I sighed. "So, when?"

"The day Ettore will die is coming very soon. I promise you. As for the angels, Domiel is on Ettore's side. Along with Munker, Bartholomew, and Arael."

"Shit," Hades growled. "How did he manage to get them on his side?"

"It seems the angels aren't happy that we had shut the veil to stop them from coming earthside," Odin explained.

"Were they always working with him?" I asked.

Odin nodded his head. "Yes. They were the ones that helped him to cross between the worlds."

"How did they cross the veil after it was closed?" Kade asked.

Odin breathed in deeply. "We have a double agent."

"What?" Hades gasped. "Who?"

I looked around the room to see if I could find any of the gods and goddesses that weren't there. Everyone seemed to be in the room.

"Anubis."

An audible gasp sounded through the crowd. One of the gods had turned against us and was working with Ettore. How many others were there?

Chapter Seven

E stesius
This was worse than I'd expected. We had heard about how evil Ettore was, and we'd known about his capture of Aphrodite, but to see that he had angels and gods now working with him was the worst-case scenario. Everyone in the room was in shocked silence. How the hell was I going to fix this?

"Where is Anubis?" Hades asked.

"He is hiding in the training center with Ettore," Odin responded.

I scrubbed my hand up over my face. It was still blowing my mind that I was sitting here amongst gods, but to know that some of them could be just as evil as Ettore was terrifying.

"How many more could be working with Ettore?" I asked.

Odin looked over at me and gave me a warm smile. "Hello, Estesius. I was honored to spend time with your father growing up. He was a very close friend."

My eyes widened, and I gasped. I never knew my father. My Mama said that he'd left after their first night together.

"Who is my father?" I asked in shock. Boyd reached out and clasped my hand. He knew my story; he knew what a horrible life I'd had and how hard it had been on my Mama to try and raise me as an outsider.

My Mama was human and had married after she gave birth to me. But I was born supernatural, while my other siblings were all human. Mama didn't know how to raise a supernatural.

Odin sighed. "I would like to talk to you more about it later, but your Papa was Poseidon."

I gasped and shared a look with Boyd. "As in the god Poseidon?" Fenris asked with shock threaded through his voice.

Odin smiled and nodded his head. "Yes. There is a lot to your story that you obviously don't know, but you will learn."

"What happened to him?" I asked.

Odin glanced over at Hades, who nodded his head. "Unfortunately, Poseidon is no longer with us. He took his own life just after your Mama fell pregnant with you."

"That's where he went? Mama thought he'd just left her," I said quietly.

"Let's talk more about this privately," Odin suggested again. I nodded my head, but there was going to be nothing more that would sink into my brain. My father was a god. What did that make me?

The meeting continued around me as everyone discussed what would happen to Ettore and the angels. They discussed what could be done about the human children that had been abducted, but my mind couldn't focus.

After the meeting ended, Odin walked over to where I sat with Boyd and Fenris; I couldn't move. Tears burned at my eyes, and my mind swirled with thoughts.

"Estesius," Odin said quietly.

I looked up at the creator and felt tears start tearing down my cheeks. "Why didn't he want to stay with my Mama? Why didn't he stay for me?"

"Oh, sweet girl. Times were different then; the gods weren't supposed to be earthside. Supernaturals were still in hiding. If it had been found out who Poseidon was, he would have been hunted down. The choice for him to leave wasn't easy, and in the end, it became too much for him. He was so in love with your Mama and wanted so desperately to be in your life."

Odin was right; the time was different when I was born. I was almost one hundred and fifty years old. I didn't look much older than twenty, which shocked most people when they found out just how old I was. My Mama had gone against the rules; she'd kept me even though she knew I was supernatural. She'd kept me hidden; I wasn't allowed outside to play with the other children, I wasn't allowed to go to school, and I was kept away from my siblings. At first, she had no idea, but when I was three, I shifted the first time, and of course, that was when Mama worked it out.

Mama did her best to treat me like I was normal, but how do you treat a child the same as the others when that child is born so differently?

"What does this mean for Estesius?" Boyd asked. Estesius wasn't even the name that Mama gave me. I chose that name when I was an adult. It actually came from a book I'd read about a Pegasus. She was the Pegasus queen, so I'd chosen to call myself Estesius. My real name was Molly. But I didn't feel like it fit.

"Estesius, you are a demi-god," Odin answered.

I gasped, and my eyes widened. "Like Aphrodite?" Boyd questioned.

Odin nodded his head. "Yes. Aphrodite was the daughter of Uranus; she was conceived after he was murdered."

My eyes widened. "What does this mean for me? I always just thought I was a Pegasus."

Odin nodded. "You are, but your powers far exceed that of a Pegasus. You chose the name Estesius after Queen Pegasus. Still, you didn't know that you, Estesius are the Queen of Pegasus." My mouth dropped open, and Odin chuckled. "This is a lot to take in, but the Pegasus council has been waiting a long time to meet you finally."

I scrubbed my hand up over my face and shook my head. "I can't. This is all too much."

Odin nodded. "I understand. Take some time; if you need more information, ask me. Don't worry about the Pegasus council; they will be there after the war. There is no hurry to see them now."

I nodded my head but remained silent. What the hell was my life like?

Chapter Eight

B oyd

"I've read the information about the gods; Poseidon died over one hundred years ago," Fenris said with a frown.

Odin nodded his head. "One hundred and forty-nine years ago, to be exact, in 1874."

Fenris's eyes widened, and he gasped as he looked over at Estesius with shock. She nodded her head. "I was born in 1873."

"Holy shit," Fenris said. "I'm only forty-eight. But wolf shifters only live for at most two hundred years. What is it for Pegasus?"

"Well, normally, it would also be about two hundred years," Odin said. "However, because Estesius is a demi-god, it makes her immortal. She can still die, but it won't be of old age."

Estesius's frown was deep on her brow, and I could see her trying to work everything out. "I didn't think I had powers other than healing and shifting."

Odin nodded his head. "Your powers are a lot stronger than the average Pegasus. You can bring people back from the dead, not just heal them. And when you are shifted, your strength is far stronger. You would find your stamina is a lot more than an average Pegasus."

"Is there anything she can do that she didn't know about?" Fenris asked.

Odin nodded his head. "Your eyes. They can kill."

We all gasped simultaneously. "How?" Estesius asked in a whisper.

"It will take practice, and you've never been put in a place to be able to do it; however, with your intention, you can kill with a look," Odin explained. "If you want to learn more about this power, I can help you learn."

Estesius's frown pulled hard on her brow. "I don't want to kill."

Odin smiled and nodded his head. "And I will never force that on you. We will need healers in this war; this is enough for you."

Estesius nodded her head. "Thank you. I don't think I could take a life."

"That's quite all right."

"Why was Poseidon on earth? How did he meet my Mama in the first place?"

Odin sighed and scratched at his chin. "Poseidon was a troubled child. As much as the humans talk about his power, his strength wasn't that of many others. And as much as gods and goddesses work as a team, he was an outcast. He was always on the outer. He was never happy and decided to leave Middle Earth and come to earthside when he became a man. At the time, we weren't supposed to leave Middle Earth. That was mostly for our safety, but Poseidon decided to risk it. When he met your mother, he fell in love instantly. However, when his father Cronus discovered that he was not only on earth but had impregnated a human, he demanded that Poseidon return to Middle Earth. But he missed your Mama greatly and was devastated that he couldn't be there to help raise you. He begged Cronus to allow him to bring you back to Middle Earth, but our fathers wouldn't allow it. That was when he committed suicide."

My eyes widened as I heard Odin speak. "Wait a minute, your father? But I thought you were the creator?" Fenris asked, thinking the same as me.

Odin chuckled. "I am. But I had to come from somewhere. My father was Borr, and my Mother was Bestla. A creator is born with every generation; there is only one. When it is time, the old creator ascends to the tree, and our child takes over. I was the creator that has taken over from my father, Borr. My son Baldur will take over from me when I'm called home."

"The tree?" I asked.

"Gods can't die. Well, that isn't exactly true, they can, but we don't die like supernaturals or humans. Instead of our heart-stopping and breathing ceasing, we disappear; we ascend. We are taken to another world called the tree of life. It is where our energy lives. If you were to look at the world as a large Oak, you could make more sense of it. The gods that ascend are the tree's roots; our energy feeds the gods; the gods are the trunk, and they give their energy to new lives. Then supernaturals and humans are the branches and leaves. When you die, your energy goes back to the trunk to keep it growing; then when a god ascends, their energy comes to the roots that feed the tree."

It was interesting. "Wow," Estesius whispered. "So, what will happen to me?"

"You will ascend to the roots," Odin replied.

"Even though I have half human?"

"You are still a goddess, regardless of who your mother was."

Estesius rubbed her hand up over her face, and she looked between the three of us. "This is mind-blowing. I never thought when we came to the Wild Claw Pack that I would not only find another mate, but I would also find out I'm a goddess."

Odin smiled warmly. "Everything happens for a reason," he replied, winking the eye that wasn't covered in a patch. He stood from where he'd been sitting and vaporized out of the atmosphere.

Estesius, Fenris, and I sat silently as we mulled over everything Odin had just explained.

"I'm a fucking goddess," Estesius said with a giggle.

"You sure are, baby, in more ways than one," I smirked, kissing her on the shoulder.

"I agree. That head game, my god," Fenris replied.

I shook my head. "Not my god. It's my goddess."

Estesius threw her head back and bellowed out a laugh before letting out a sigh. "Well, come on, I suppose we should find out what we will be expected to do about these humans that Ettore has abducted."

Chapter Nine

F enris

    Estesius lay between Boyd and me in my bed; our bodies were sweaty from the sex we'd just finished.

"What are we going to do once this is all over?" Estesius asked.

"What do you mean?" Boyd asked.

"Well, when this war is over, what is going to happen to us?" she said, pointing between Boyd and me.

"I've been giving it a little bit of thought. I will ask Craig if he wants to move the pack to Lalbert. I can see that the pack would do a lot better here, the magic here is so strong, and there are many more supernaturals here than in Portsea."

Estesius nodded her head. "I think that would be great. I'm feeling a little bit overwhelmed by everything."

"I can imagine," I said as I skimmed my hand up and down Estesius's naked spine. It had been a hell of a time the last two days from realizing that Estesius and Boyd were my mates to discovering that Estesius is a demi-god and Ettore's attack on humans.

Not to mention finding out that Anubis and some angels were working with Ettore. Odin had hinted that it might not be the only god working with Ettore, which worried me.

"I guess I knew that life was about to get hectic," Estesius said.

"But you've learned a lot about yourself very quickly," I noted.

Estesius giggled and nodded her head. "For sure."

I heard my front door open, and Connell called my name. "I'll be right out," I called. I chuckled and climbed out of bed, slipping my jeans on.

"No worries," Connell replied with humor in his voice. Estesius and Boyd climbed out of bed and quickly put clothes back on before following me to the living room. "It was so much easier finding my mate in prison. We could fuck without too much interruption. Sorry."

I chuckled and shook my head. "Don't worry. We get it."

Connell's smile dropped slightly as he gave a sigh. "Kade wants to rescue the human kids."

I winced. "How is he planning on doing that?"

"He wants to send Posus and Negus in with Forest and River to rescue them."

My eyes widened. I could understand Connell's concern, especially sending his son Posus in. But no adults were being sent in.

"Who are they?" Boyd asked.

"Posus is my son, Negus, Forest, and River are other children from the Devil's Advocates."

"They want to send kids in?" Estesius asked.

Connell nodded his head. "Posus can blend in with the shadows and hide, while Negus can hold invisibility. Forest and River are strong and carry poison in their spit."

"I understand Posus and Negus but not Forest and River," I said.

"Kade is in the dining hall with Anghus and the inner Devils if you want to come with me and talk to him."

I nodded and glanced over at Estesius and Boyd, who nodded. We left the house and went over to the dining hall. Kade was sitting in a chair at one of the long tables with Anghus, Israel, Jai, Jasper, Arley, Zion, Oakland, Scout, Hawke, and a few of the AJE authority shifter unit and Lucifer.

"Hey, come and sit down so we can go over the plan," Kade said.

I sat beside Anghus, making room for Estesius and Boyd to sit beside me.

"Okay, so here is what I know. The abducted kids are being held in an abandoned building guarded by alphas in Ettore's army. My vampire team was able to count fifteen alphas. The building is on Smith St, one of the last closest to the river."

"Are all the buildings there still abandoned?" Anghus asked.

Kade nodded his head. "Yeah, they are; that is probably why Ettore decided to put them there."

"Is this another trap?" I asked.

Kade sighed and shrugged his shoulders. "I don't know. It could be, but I don't think it is. I think now that Kade has Anubis and the angels, he is feeling overconfident."

"So, what are you suggesting we do?" Memphis asked.

"My thought is that we create a bit of a red herring. If we make it look like we are about to raid the training facility, it will direct his attention to that, and then we can get into the building and get the kids out," Kade said.

I nodded my head, but the plan sounded too simple. I wondered if Ettore would fall for it.

"So, what kind of distraction are you going to do?"

"I'm going to send my vampire team, the shifter unit, the witch team, Lucifer, Hades, and Hel. The vampires, shifters, and witches will staff the outside while Lucifer, Hades, and Hel enter the building. They will cause a commotion there; at the same time, I want to send Negus and Posus into the abandoned building with Aithan and Gumma. Aithan, Negus, and Posus can get into the building without being seen; Gumma can then get the kids out by transporting them through space to the precinct."

"Are you going to have others arrest the alphas there?" Connell asked.

Kade shook his head. "No. I know that none of us want death, but this war is. Those alphas are casualties of war."

I winced. I hated it but understood. If we let them live, they would go straight back to Ettore, and we would not hit his army.

"How are you planning on killing them?" Lynx asked.

"That is where your sons will come in. Forest and River will go with Hera; her powers will increase the potency of the boy's poison, and they will use their poison like a blow dart."

"I don't want my kids being responsible for people's deaths. Do you know what that will do to their mind?" Lynx argued.

Kade sighed and nodded his head. "I had a feeling you might say that. The only other way we can do it is to send Hera alone."

"Yes, do that," Lynx growled. "Fuck, even I'll go. But I'm not sending my kids to murder someone."

"What do you think they are going to have to do when this war is in full flight?" the leader of the Whitetail pack, Tasha, snapped.

Lynx spun on the wolf shifter and glared. "I will protect my sons; they are not assassins."

"If you don't teach them to take a life, then you will lose them, damn it. This isn't a time to wrap our kids in cotton wool," Tasha spat back.

Lynx punched his hand into the table. "I said no. They are my fucking children, and fuck you for thinking I should be okay with my kids murdering people."

"Enough," Kade growled. "Your kids don't have to kill anyone. We will send Hera in."

"I will go too," Estesius said.

I gasped, and my eyes widened. "Baby, no," Boyd said.

Estesius nodded her head. "We can't let the alphas live; if they live, they will return to Ettore, and his army will be just as strong."

"You don't know how to use your powers yet," I argued.

Estesius shrugged her shoulders. "I will learn."

Chapter Ten

E stesius
   If I was to say I wasn't nervous, I would be lying. I never thought there would be a day I would have to kill another person. But I understood there were rare times. This was part of war; if I didn't toughen up, I wouldn't survive.

"Are you sure you want to do this?" Fenris asked. I knew that he and Boyd were nervous about this mission.

"I don't want to do it, but I know I need to."

"Hera can go in alone," Fenris argued.

"I know she can. But this is part of the war, Fenris. I hate that people have to die, but the fact is that it is part of the war."

Fenris sighed and scrubbed his hand up over his face. "I fucking hate it."

I smiled, reached out my hand, and stroked it over his arm. "I know, sweetheart, I know. I hate war, but when I agreed to come with Boyd, I knew there was a reason for it."

Fenris pulled me into his arms and pressed his lips hard against mine. I moaned and thrust my hands through his hair as our tongues tangled. I was breathless when Fenris pulled back and looked down into my eyes.

"Be fucking safe and come home to me."

I smiled. "If you kiss me like that again, there is nowhere I would rather be."

Fenris chuckled and pressed his head to my forehead. "I love you."

My eyes widened, and I gasped. "You've only known me for four days."

Fenris smirked. "And yet I just know."

"I love you too," I responded.

"Are you ready?" Hera asked from behind me. I turned to face the goddess and nodded my head. The last two days had been spent learning how to use my powers. It was actually quite terrifying. My eyes didn't just kill; they completely disintegrated.

"I'm ready," I answered as I moved away from Fenris and pressed my lips quickly to Boyd's. He was watching me with concern all over his face. We had a huge argument the night I'd agreed to go in. I knew he didn't want me to go, but I couldn't express it enough; this was war.

"Come home," Boyd growled.

I nodded my head and smiled. "Always."

I walked away with nervousness in my belly. "It will be fine," Hera assured me, but I couldn't be sure. We joined with Aithan, Iver, Negus, Posus, and Gumma; reaching out, I took hold of Hera and Gumma's hand and felt the world tilt as we started to move through the atmosphere. When we stopped, I looked around to see that we were standing behind a large factory.

"The property is the next one over," Aithan explained.

Hera nodded her head. "Estesius and I will go in first; the vampire team has reported two at the front, two at the back, and the rest inside the building. If we cause commotion at the front, that will chase the alphas out toward us. That will open the back for you to get in and get the kids out."

Aithan nodded his head before turning to the kids. "Ready?"

"Yes," Iver answered as he reached out and took hold of Gummas. Together the kids all disappeared into the shadows.

"Let's go," Hera instructed. I nodded my head and took her hand. Hera moved through the atmosphere, dropping us in front of the two alphas manning the door. Their eyes widened, and they gasped as we appeared in front of them.

I narrowed my eyes and glared at one of the alphas. Instantly he screeched, and his body started to smoke. It happened so quickly he didn't even have time to pull his weapon. The other alpha cried out as Hera spat acidic poison in his face, and his body began to melt. The vision made me shudder. It was horrific, so much worse than I could imagine. But I didn't have time to dwell on it as more alphas came running around the building.

I turned to face them and shot each alpha as they rounded the corner of the building. Instantly they turned to ash in front of me with an ear-piercing scream. Behind me, Hera was melting the other alphas.

"That's all of them," Hera announced once the last of the alpha's died. I nodded my head and moved to the front of the building. We went through each room, but every space was empty.

"They've moved the kids," I said with relief. My entire body was shaking, and I felt sick to my stomach.

I couldn't even start to think about the fact that we'd just killed people. The thought made me sick. I was a murderer. Was it murder in the name of war?

Chapter Eleven

B oyd
I was pacing back and forth across the floor of the house we were staying in with Fenris. I fucking hated it. I'd yelled and screamed until my voice was hoarse, trying to stop Estesius from going in. I knew she could protect herself, but that wasn't what worried me; it was what killing someone would do to her. Our pack had been peaceful. We weren't like some packs that fought for leadership. We were a family and had made peace and love the most important values at Palecrest.

The fact that Estesius had volunteered to kill people made me feel sick. I hated the thought of it. But she was determined. She made a good point; this was war. I understood that. We would probably all have to take a life at some stage throughout the war, but it didn't make me happier. I don't know what I thought when I agreed to help in this war. I knew that there would be death. I guess I just thought I could protect my mate from it.

"They are back," Fenris said as he looked out the window.

I turned and rushed out of the door; the kids were standing in the center square with the human children, many of who were crying and obviously scared. Hera and Estesius arrived just as I reached the court.

"Estesius," I growled as I pulled her into my arms and held her tight.

"I told you I'd come back," she said quietly.

The look on her face was what I'd feared. She was feeling guilty. She wasn't dealing with what she had just done. I cupped her cheeks and looked down into her eyes, which were quickly welling with tears.

"Estesius, look," Iver said, drawing my mate's attention. "See these children? You saved them. Each of these girls was going to be raped. The boys would be tortured and used as experiments to train other alphas. You saved them."

The tears streaked down Estesius's cheeks as a sob fell from her life. "Those alphas, though, they were innocents."

Iver shook his head. "No. They weren't. Those alphas were all demons; they joined Ettore in the underworld. They were there by their own free will."

Estesius's eyes widened, and she gasped. "Really?"

Iver smiled and nodded his head. "Yes. The alphas he is still training he doesn't trust to guard because he is scared that they will realize what he is doing is wrong. That's why Ettore only uses the demons or those that joined him willingly."

Estesius let out a small breath. "So, I didn't kill anyone innocent?"

"No, Estesius, you didn't. Those men were going to rape these girls, and they would be put in charge of torturing the boys. Those men were as evil as Ettore himself."

Estesius ran her hands up over her face and nodded her head. "Thank you, Iver."

He smiled. "Please talk it out, don't let that guilt eat you up. You have a little one who will need her Mama."

My eyes widened, and my mouth dropped open just as Estesius and Fenris gasped from either side of me.

"I'm pregnant?" Estesius asked quietly.

Iver chuckled. "You are."

The tears that had dried in Estesius's eyes started to fall again; this time though they weren't tears of anguish, they were tears of happiness. She turned back to face Fenris and me. "I'm pregnant," she cried.

Fenris and I pulled Estesius into our arms and held her tight against us. I couldn't explain my feelings. My head was spinning. We had wanted a child for so long now. And finally, we were about to have one. The downside was that this child would be born into a time of war.

"I'm gonna be a Papa," Fenris crowed, making me and Estesius laugh.

I wrapped my arm around Fenris's neck and kissed his lips passionately, making him moan.

"Children, here," Iver roared, making Fenris laugh against my lips.

"What is going to happen to these children?" Estesius asked.

Iver sighed. "Those with families will go to them, but two don't have a biological family, so they will go into foster care."

I frowned and shook my head. "Would we be able to foster them?"

Iver shrugged his shoulder. Being human, I don't know how the law works. "The best person to ask would be Kade; he could put you in contact with the proper authorities. Normally if they were supernatural children, they would stay with the Devil's, Onyx Rebels, or Wild Claw Pack. Still, for humans, I don't know."

"Do you think we should look at fostering the children?" I nodded my head. "What do you think?" I said, turning to Estesius and Fenris.

Estesius nodded her head. "Yes. I don't know what human foster care is like, but it has to be just as bad as supernatural foster care."

"Yeah, that's what I was thinking too." Not that I knew anything about the foster care system. I was fortunate; Craig and I grew up very well-loved and protected. But I hated the idea that these children who had been through a traumatic event would be sent to live with strangers who might hurt them further.

"I agree; let's go and talk to Kade," Fenris said.

Kade was standing with the children, with a few women, one I recognized as Arcadia, the dragon shifter record keeper. I took hold of Estesius's hand and walked toward them.

"Thank you, Estesius," Kade said as he noticed us.

Estesius smiled and nodded her head. "You don't have to thank me. It was the right thing to do. I would like to talk to you, though. Iver suggested that two children without biological families would be placed in foster care. What can we do to foster them?"

Arcadia smiled and placed her hand on her chest. "Thank the gods," she said. "I was worried about them. I will work through the paperwork with you; Michael, the social worker, will be here in a few minutes. The children will all be spending the night in the hospital, but there should be no reason why we can't get you through as foster parents for them."

I smiled. That was perfect. At least I knew the children would be safe with us. We would protect them, and Ettore would never be able to get to the children again.

"This is Brandon and Langley," Kade said as he brought two children. "Brandon is twelve, and Langley is six. They are biological brothers and sisters. This is Estesius, Boyd and Fenris. Boyd and Fenris are wolf shifters, and Estesius is a Pegasus. They are going to be the ones that will be fostering you. What do you think?"

Langley's eyes lit up, and she looked at her brother before turning back to us. "Can you shift into a wolf and a pretty horse?"

Estesius smiled and nodded her head. "I can; I have big wings too. My main is purple, and my body's fur sparkles like glitter."

Langley giggled. "Can I see?"

"Sure, you can," Estesius said as she stepped back. I watched as the air around her rippled, and suddenly she shifted from human to the beautiful Pegasus that she was. Langley's eyes were wide, and even Brandon looked impressed.

"Can I pat her?" Langley asked.

"Of course you can," I replied with a smile.

Langley reached out her hand, and Estesius came forward, lowering her head to the little girl. Langley stroked down over Estesius's nose and smiled. Tears welled in the little girl's eyes, and she turned back to Brandon.

"Do you want to live here, Brandon?"

Brandon was quiet, but he gave a quick head nod. He stuffed his hands in his pockets, and I could tell how angry he was. I didn't blame him. His family had been killed, and he'd been abducted.

"I would be thrilled to have you both here; there is a lot for you to do," Fenris said.

Brandon looked up at him and shrugged his shoulders with a sigh. "You'll only want us here until we age out."

I frowned and cocked my head to the side. "What makes you say that?"

Brandon's eyes were wet with tears when he looked at me. "No one wants us for very long."

"I'm sorry that people have mistreated you, Brandon, and made you think that. But I can promise you that once you are part of the Palecrest Pack or the Wild Claw Pack, you are family for life. We don't turn our backs on family."

Chapter Twelve

F enris

"Welcome, Langley and Brandon," Amos said as we walked into the school building on the Devil's Advocates compound. The kids had been living with us for two weeks and were ready to start school.

Langley had taken to living amongst supernaturals, but Brandon had been hesitant. He was angry and untrusting. We learned through Michael and Arcadia that the people they had been living with were foster parents. The kids had been through hell. They were taken from their biological mother when Langley was only a few weeks old. Apparently, the mother was a drug addict and sex worker. Brandon had been left at home alone with his newborn sister. He'd tried to give her a bottle, but he'd heated it too high in the microwave and burned Langley's mouth. In a panic, he ran to the neighbor and admitted what he had done. The neighbor rang the police and ambulance, and the kids were taken into care while their mother was imprisoned for child neglect.

From there, the kids were moved from home to home. They never last more than a few weeks at most places. It was really heartbreaking. Michael told us their mother had her parenting rights removed, so we could adopt the children if we wanted to. Of course, we wanted to, but we sat Brandon and Langley down to ask them if they wanted something. Brandon sobbed like a baby when he realized he would have a forever home. My heart broke for him as I held him tight and soothed his tears.

The very next day, we went through all the paperwork, it would be a few more weeks until it was finalized, but we couldn't wait. It was time to give the kids as much structure and stability as possible. Well, in wartime, anyway.

"My name is Amos; I'm the special needs teacher, but let me introduce you to your teachers. Langley, this is Miss Schilling; she will be your teacher along with Canea, Posus, Lucida, and Parker. Brandon, this is Mr. Donner; he will be your teacher along with some of the older kids here; there are too many of them for me to list them," Amos said with a laugh.

"Langley," Canea called out when she spotted the girl that had become her best friend.

"Canea, I'm going to be in your class now," Langley replied with a wide smile. Canea wrapped her arms around her friend and brought her into the classroom to show her everything.

"Fenris?" Brandon said as he looked at me with a slight frown pulling at his brow.

"Yes, mate?" I replied.

"I'm human, all the other kids are supernatural, and I know they are learning about their powers; what will I do?"

"I can answer that," Anghus said as he came in behind us. "We have been thinking about this, and if you would like, the decision is yours, but as much as the kids learn about their powers, we also teach them fighting and working with weapons. While the kids are working on their powers, I thought maybe you and I could spend some time together, and I can teach you some self-defense and how to fight. Hawke, who you haven't met yet, works with weapons, like swords, blades, and staffs, and can teach you that too."

Brandon's eyes widened, and a small smile touched his lips. He glanced over at me, and I gave him a wink and nodded my head. "Is that something you'd like to do?" I asked.

Brandon nodded enthusiastically. "Yes, please."

Anghus grinned and laid a big hand on the boy's shoulder. "Excellent. I look forward to it."

"Thank you, Anghus," he said just as Iver came in and put his arm around Brandon's shoulder. All the kids looked up to Iver, and he protected them.

"Iver," Brandon said with a grin as he looked up at the older boy.

"Hey, I'm glad you are starting school with us today."

"Your Dad said I could learn fighting while you are learning about your powers."

Iver grinned and nodded his head. "That's awesome. If you want, we can practice sparring sometimes to practice."

"Really? You'd do that with me?"

Iver nodded. "Of course, I would. You're family now."

Brandon's mouth dropped open, looking over at me with wide eyes. "I'm family," he whispered.

"You sure are," I replied, scrubbing my hand over his hair.

Chapter Thirteen

E stesius

"Thank you, everyone, for coming," Kade said as we gathered in the large hall on the Devil's Advocates compound. "I'm pleased we successfully got all the kids out of the factory two weeks ago. The children housed with their families are safe, and the gods awarded their homes. Ettore won't be able to get to them again."

I felt relief. It had taken me a while to get it into my head that the men I'd killed were terrible and they deserved their death, but it finally settled. Mainly when I talked to Brandon and Langley and found out what the kids had been through. Unfortunately, we had been too late, and some of the girls had been raped already. Thankfully, Langley wasn't one of them, but my heart broke for the girls that had.

"I'm going to turn this over to Lucifer now so that he can explain what happened when he entered the training facility," Kade said before stepping to the side as Lucifer took center stage.

"As we thought, Domiel, Munker, Bartholomew, and Arael were there working with Ettore. They, however, are no longer living. My presence at the training center was like a cat among pigeons. There were a lot of panic. Ettore is still in charge, but his mind has gone so far that he is no longer leaving the training center. From what I discovered, he is basically bedridden, and Blaise Knight and Vex Blakely, along with Anubis running the show. Anubis escaped as I killed the angels; unfortunately, he is still alive. This war is coming very soon; I would suggest in the next few months as I could feel that Blaise, Vex, and Anubis are assembling the troops ready to go."

"Are there any other gods or goddesses working with Ettore?" Anghus asked.

Lucifer shook his head. "No. Anubis is working on his own. He is scared and hiding his best from Odin. But now he knows we are aware, so I suspect he will keep a low profile. However, Anubis will die before this war takes place."

"Is that where Ettore has been getting his power?" Bacchus asked.

Lucifer nodded his head. "It was Anubis that helped him to capture Aphrodite. We have verified that Anubis has been working with Ettore for over millennia. He was the one that helped Ettore gain rulership in the underworld. Anubis altered the minds of the demons, making way for Ettore to take over. However, Ettore was just a pawn in Anubis's game. I don't know that Ettore will live or die very soon."

"So, has it always been Anubis that wanted this war?" Connell asked.

Lucifer shook his head. "Oh no, Ettore very much wanted this war. His plan was to gain the powers of Anubis and then kill him, too and take over. However, the difference is that Aphrodite was a demi-god, and her powers weren't as strong as Anubis's. Ettore's mind cannot handle the power of a god, which is why he is now losing his mind. Too much power will kill him."

The atmosphere rippled, and Odin stepped on the stage. I gasped in horror as I looked at Odin's hand. He lifted it above his head before dropping the head he held in his hand. The head bounced onto the floor and rolled, coming to a halt in front of Odin. The mouth of the head was in a full grimace, and the milky eyes stared vacantly at the crowd.

"Anubis is dead," Odin sneered. "Let this be known to all of the gods and goddesses in this room; I will destroy any of you that try to hurt my people."

With that, the atmosphere rippled again and Odin, along with Anubis's head, blinked out as if they had never been there. I turned and stared at my mates in shock. Had I just imagined that? The look on my mate's face told me I hadn't.

"Well, that happened," Kade said with a laugh. "I guess we don't have to worry about Anubis anymore."

"Yeah," Lucifer said with shock. "Um, well, that's all I have."

"I think maybe we might call it for now," Kade replied. "Thank you, everyone, for coming."

Nobody said a word as we all stared at what had just happened. But it made me realize just how easy life was given and how quickly it was taken.

Chapter Fourteen

B oyd

Odin's actions were the talk of the pack lands. We were all in shock. Not that he'd killed Anubis but the anger that came from him. When we were growing up and taught about the gods, I guessed we'd been taught they were loving and kind. But there was nothing loving or kind in the way Odin killed Anubis. I didn't feel sorry for Anubis; he dug his grave when he teamed up with Ettore.

Knowing that Ettore was bedridden and going crazy, in one sense, was comforting. But it was also anti-climactic. I wanted to see him die on the battlefield. I wondered what would happen the day he died. Would this war just fizzle away? Were we all gearing up for nothing? That would be great, but on the other hand, it would suck, especially for those that had already lost their lives. They died for nothing.

"Boyd," Craig yelled as he came running into the house with horror on his face.

"What?" I said, feeling panic grip me; something was wrong.

"He's taken Estesius."

"Who? Who has taken her?" I roared.

"Ettore, well, not Ettore but someone involved with him."

"No," I growled. My wolf howled. Fenris came running up the path simultaneously as I stormed out of the house.

"We've got eyes on them; Vex Blakely got her. She was in Lalbert, and he grabbed her from the front of a café. Tabby, who owns the place, rang Kade; Arcadia was able to get out and follow them."

"Where is he taking her?" I asked. My heart was pounding hard in my chest. This was my mate; I couldn't stand the thought of anyone taking her. This could be a trap, a way to get us to go to Ettore, to kill us, but I would die for my mate. I would walk through the doors of hell and crossfire to protect her.

"Kade believes that he is taking her to the house that Ettore owns; it is trapped with spikes and all sorts of booby traps."

"I don't care what traps there are; I'm going in," I snarled as I ran to the car; I wasn't going to wait. By the time I'd climbed into the driver's seat, Fenris was climbing into the passenger side.

"We will go in," he said.

I nodded and brought the car to life, moving out of the pack lands. When I reached the road, I heard the roar of engines as many of the Wild Claw Pack, and Devil's Advocates joined us. My heart was ricocheting against my ribs, and my hands were sweating. Please, please, fight, baby.

"Pull over on the dirt road up there; I think there is a trap waiting for us; we have to go in quietly," Fenris directed.

I nodded my head and pulled the car up on a dirt road that was surrounded by forest. The bikes stopped behind us. Anghus, Jasper, and Jai came toward us. "We will shift and fly over the top of the house, I can see Arcadia high in the sky, so I'd say that Ettore knows we are onto him," Anghus explained.

I nodded my head. Another car pulled up behind us, and Kade climbed out of the driver's side; two of the Onyx Rebels followed him, Hawke and Scout.

"Okay, what is happening?" Kade asked.

"We are going to go up high and watch the house. Hawke and Scout, can you go low to the house in the canopy and tell us what you see and the wolves and shifters who can go through the forest? But beware that there are traps," Anghus said.

Kade nodded, and those who were shifting started to strip from their clothes. I wanted to barrel in and destroy the place, but I knew I had to be innovative. Before we could shift, I screamed so loud sounded through the air. I gasped and stared up into the sky from the sound's direction. A colossal dragon lifted into the air, its skin as dark as night.

"It's Vex," Kade growled.

Vex turned his head and stared at us. He turned in the sky and started to fly toward us. "Get into the forest," Anghus roared.

I called my wolf forward and ran into the canopy of the trees. I looked up into the canopy and watched as Vex flew over the top of the forest and spat fire at the trees. The trees exploded under the heat. A heat I'd never felt surrounded me, and my wolf howled.

"Shit," Fenris roared. "Run."

All the wolf shifters took off at a run, moving as fast as we could to get out of the fire. Another screech sounded through the air, and when I looked up through the gap in the canopy, I watched as Arcadia's dragon swooped down close to Vex, drawing his attention to her.

"She is going to keep him distracted," Kade said through the link we were all connected to.

"We will fly through the canopy and see if we can see Estesius," Scout said.

We stood together, wolves, vampires, a gargoyle, chimera, and griffon, watching Arcadia and Vex trading fire and blows. I couldn't tell who was winning; Arcadia gave as good as she got. Both dragons were bleeding and were wounded.

"I've got her," Hawke announced through the link. "I'm going to lead her through to you now."

My heart slowed, and relief washed over me. We weren't out of danger yet, but at least, as far as I knew, Estesius would be safe.

Chapter Fifteen

E stesius

"Thank you, Tabby; the kids are going to love these," I said with a smile. Ada, who I'd met yesterday, told me about Tabbies café and I couldn't wait to try it. The kids had been doing fantastically at school. They had been there for two months, and we had just received information that the adoption was going to go through, so I'd come to Tabbies to get some cakes to celebrate with.

Tabby smiled and gave me a wave as I left the shop. The days started getting warmer as summer found its way to Australia. I pulled my sunglasses off the top of my head and pulled my keys from my bag as I headed toward the car.

Suddenly I felt two hands grab me hard, and I was lifted without thought. I screamed and started to kick back at the person holding me.

"Shut the fuck up, cunt," a man growled in my ear.

I turned my head as I tried to look into his eyes to use my powers, but something was stopping it. I tried shifting, but my Pegasus wasn't there. I didn't understand what was going on. The only way for that to happen was to use silver. I realized as I looked down that the man wore silver gloves.

"Let me go," I screamed, hoping someone would do something if I drew enough attention.

The man continued to staff handle and threw me into the back of a car before slamming the door shut. I reached out and tried to open the doors, but it was locked. I focused on drawing my Pegasus forward, but nothing happened.

"Don't even try; this whole car is coated in silver," the man chuckled as he turned to look at me.

Vex Blakely. Shit. I'd been kidnapped by Vex Blakely.

"What do you want with me?" I begged.

"I don't want you, but you are needed."

I frowned and shook my head. "For what?"

"You'll see. Now shut the fuck up," he growled as he started the engine on the car and started to drive.

I didn't know if this would be the last day on earth. I rubbed my hand down over my belly. It only just started to protrude. All my checkups with the goddess Diana said our little girl was growing well. She was healthy and robust. But I had no idea what Vex was planning to do with me.

I wondered if this was payback for what I did to the demons. Or if it was because I was a demi-god. Had Anubis told Ettore that before he died. Tears streamed down my cheeks. I was helpless. The silver made all of my powers useless. I didn't really know how to fight, not to mention how much bigger Vex was than me. If it came to a physical fight, I wouldn't be able to win.

It felt like forever before we were pulled into the forest and down a dirt road. The canopy of the trees hung over the road, blocking any light. The deeper into the woods we went, the darker it became.

"Good," Vex chuckled.

I looked up at him, but he didn't say anything more before turning into a driveway to an abandoned house. As soon as he turned the car off, he climbed out. I got myself ready. I might not have been able to use my powers, but I would fight with everything I had.

The minute that Vex opened the door, I launched my attack. I tore out of the car with a scream and clawed at his face. Vex roared and stepped back. His lapse in concentration was enough for me to be able to run. I took off before turning my head to use my powers. However, Vex was faster than I'd been expecting. He was right behind me; he'd swung his fist back hard and slammed it into the center of my face.

My eyes rolled, and I groaned as darkness washed over me, sucking me under. I felt my knees wobble and collapse just as the night took over. When I awoke again, I was inside a room with a bed, and that was it. The windows had been bricked over, and the door was shut.

I stood from the bed and ran to the door. I tried the knob and found that it was unlocked. As quietly as possible, I cracked the door and looked out into a hallway. Not seeing Vex anyone, I opened the door wider and started to move through the doorway into the hall. It opened as I was about to open the front door, and I sucked in a deep breath, ready to call my power forward and kill Vex. But it wasn't Vex that came into the room. Instead, it was Hawke.

"You're safe; I've got you," Hawke said. A sob fell from my lips, and I nodded my head. "Are you alone?"

"I think so; Vex Blakely was the one that took me."

Hawke nodded his head. "I know; he is fighting Arcadia at the moment. Let's get you out of here and to safety."

My eyes widened. Hawke reached out, took my hand, and pulled me through the door into the forest. I could hear the screeches of Arcadia and Vex coming from the sky. I didn't dare to look up as I ran through the woods with Hawke.

Eventually, we came out of the forest beside a group of cars and bikes. "Estesius," Boyd cried.

I looked up just as he appeared from the forest and pulled me into his arms. "I'm alright, I'm alright," I said.

Boyd frowned and shook his head. "You're not; you're bruised."

I touched my face gingerly and shrugged. "It's nothing," I said as another screech sounded through the sky. I looked up to see Arcadia's dragon falling through the sky toward the ground. I gasped.

Without a second thought, I shifted and took off into the sky. I heard Boyd roar my name, but there was no stopping me. I flew as fast as I could toward Vex. My eyes were narrowed, and he was zeroed in on my sights.

The closer I got to him, the more I realized how hurt he was. His dragon was bleeding badly, and one wing was struggling to move. I sneered as I approached him.

"Vex," I snarled, drawing the dragon's attention.

The dragon turned to face me, and without any other warning, I pushed my power forward. The dragon screamed an unholy screech as his body erupted into flames. Soot, ash, and flames flew off in all directions, carried in the wind. I hovered in the sky, watching as the last of his body disappeared into the atmosphere before flying down to where I could see Arcadia's dragon.

When I landed, the others were already around her. Kade was trying to give her blood, but it was too late. She was dead. I shifted back to my human body and kneeled beside the dragon. Resting my hand on her chest, I focused on Arcadia's aura. The gold atmosphere wrapped around my hand, and I watched as Arcadia's spirit lifted from her body.

"Do you want to go back to your body?" I asked.

Arcadia smiled and nodded her head. "Yes. My job isn't done yet."

I smiled and nodded. "Go back," I directed. Arcadia's spirit was sucked back into the dragon's body beneath my hand.

Her body started to shift and alter, and the dragon shrunk, leaving Arcadia's human body in its place, healed of all wounds. Her eyes blinked open, and she slowly sat up.

"Thank you," she said with a smile.

"You're welcome."

"Where is Vex?" she asked.

"Dead."

"Best news ever," she replied with a laugh.

"You can say that again, girl," Kade said with a laugh.

Chapter Sixteen

Fenris

"Can you tell me exactly what happened?" Kade asked Estesius while we sat in the main house's living room on the Devil's Advocates compound.

"I'd just come out of Tabbies; I wasn't paying attention, which was stupid. I'd almost got to my car when Vex grabbed hold of me. He had silver gloves on, which stopped me from being able to use my powers. He'd carried me to his car and shoved me in the back. I tried to use my powers again, but I couldn't. That's when he told me that the car was encased in silver. He drove me out to the house, and when he opened the door, I'd run, but he caught me and punched me in the face, knocking me out. When I came to was when Hawke came in through the front door."

Kade nodded his head. "Did he say anything to you?"

Estesius frowned and nodded. "Yeah. He said he didn't want me, but I was needed. When I asked him what I needed, he told me I'd see. After that, he didn't talk to me again."

Kade hummed and shook his head. "I wonder what that meant."

"Could it be because she is a demi-god? Anubis possibly told Ettore or Vex, and they decided after Anubis was killed they would take another," Boyd questioned.

Kade nodded. "Yeah, that's probably it. Diana is waiting to check you over and ensure the baby is fine. How are you feeling now?"

"I'm fine," Estesius said. "As soon as I shifted, the pain and bruising in my face were gone."

"Good, go and see Diana and just get the baby checked over and take a break; you used a lot of power today." I stood with Estesius and Boyd by my side and went to the door. "And Estesius? Thank you."

Estesius smiled and nodded her head. "It is my role. You don't have to thank me."

"You saved Arcadia's life, which means more to me than you realize."

58

I cocked my head to the side. I'd assumed that only Merza was Kade's mate, but I wondered if Arcadia was perhaps his mate. I knew they were all close, but I didn't think they were mated. Not that it was any of my business.

Estesius smiled and nodded her head before she turned and led us out of the building. We walked over to the medical unit on the compound and stepped inside.

"Good afternoon; you've had a hectic day," Larissa said with a chuckle.

"You can say that again," Estesius laughed. "I've been ordered to come and see Diana to make sure the baby is doing alright."

"Of course, come on through; she is in the office," Larissa answered, guiding us through the office where Diana was waiting.

"Estesius, come on in and hop up on the bed so I can show you this little one," she said with a bright smile.

Estesius moved over to the bed and lay down. I took the seat on one side while Boyd took the other side.

"Would you like to bring the other children in so they can see their little sister?" Diana asked.

My eyes widened, and I shared a look with Estesius and Boyd. "They can see her?" Estesius asked.

"Sure, they can," Diana said with a bright smile.

Boyd nodded his head. "That would be fantastic."

"I'll go and get them," Larissa said as she left the room.

"Is the baby alright?" I asked Diana.

"Oh yes, she is doing really well and thriving," she answered.

The smile on Estesius's face was brilliant. "And we are definitely having a little girl?"

"You sure are. Have you thought of any names yet?"

Estesius nodded her head. We had been going over names since we discovered that she was pregnant. It was funny, though; the one name we had all agreed on at once was that for a little girl.

"Yes, we are going to call her Aretha."

"A perfect name. Did you know it means righteous and excellence?"

"No, I didn't know that," I said.

Diane chuckled and nodded her head. "Your daughter is destined for great things. Would you like to know what supernatural she is going to be?"

My eyes widened, and I nodded my head. "Let's wait until the kids are here," Estesius suggested.

"Good idea," Boyd answered.

We didn't have to wait long before the kids came into the room with Larissa behind them. "Are we really going to be able to see the baby?" Langley asked.

"Yes, Diana is going to show us," I replied.

Langley climbed onto the bed beside Estesius and laid her head on Estesius's chest. The little girl had become so close to Estesius; she loved nothing more than cuddling close.

"Okay, ready? Watch the wall," Diana instructed.

I turned my head to the wall and focused as an image of my daughter formed on the wall. It was a complete three-dimensional image. She had her eyes closed and her thumb in her mouth. I could tell she wasn't a fully developed baby yet, but there was no question that this was a baby.

"That's our baby," Brandon gasped as he looked at the wall. I scrubbed my hand down over the boy's hair and smiled. Tears welled in his eyes. "I'm going to protect her."

"You are an amazing big brother to Langley, so I know you will be equally as amazing to Aretha," I replied.

Brandon gave me a smile. He came out of his shell a little more every day he was with us. He was a deep thinker and carried the world on his shoulders. He loved hard and was fiercely protective of everyone he loved. But beneath all that was a sweet boy with a heart of gold.

"Now, would you like to know what kind of supernatural Aretha is?" Diana asked.

"Yes, please," Boyd answered.

"She is a simurgh."

My eyes widened, and I looked over at Boyd and Estesius, who had the same confusion on their face. I shook my head. "I've never heard of a simurgh."

Diana smiled. "That's probably because they are a highly secretive species of supernatural. Their closest relationship is the phoenix. But the simurgh originate in Persia. They live in a tiny part of Iran, in a town called Makhunik. The simurgh is generally a lot smaller than an average person. Humans would say they have dwarfism, but it is just the stature of the simurgh. They shift into a bird similar to that a phoenix. And have powers of death in their eyes, like you do, Estesius. However, they also have the power of healing."

"Wow," I whispered.

"She will be expected to fight, won't she?" Estesius said sadly.

Diana smiled and shook her head. "There is no reason she needs to fight. But she will be strong. As will be all the new generation of supernaturals. They are all strong and rare. This is a new world that she is entering. A world where people like the simurgh don't have to hide."

"I like the sound of that," I said.

"Me too," Diana replied with a smile.

Chapter Seventeen

B^{oyd} "Thank you, everyone, for coming," I said as we stood in the large dining hall. The tables were covered in a banquet of party food. Everyone had a drink. Estesius, Fenris, and I stood at the front of the room with Brandon and Langley by our side. "We wanted to have you all join us in celebrating the official adoption of Brandon and Langley. They are now our children." I held up the adoption certificates.

Everyone cheered, and Brandon and Langley's smile was wide. "Congratulations," Anghus called.

"Everyone enjoy, eat up, and party. It's time to celebrate," Fenris called.

Another roar sounded, and everyone turned to start piling their plates with food. "Go on, kids, go and grab yourselves some food."

Brandon and Langley took off to where the other kids were all sitting and settled in between them. Canea wrapped her arm around Langley and hugged her while Brandon slid in beside Forest and River. I couldn't have been happier. The kids had been the most amazing children I'd ever met. Every day they came out of their shell a little more.

Even though they were humans, they definitely had the spirit of the supernatural. Brandon had taken to learning how to fight like a fish to water. He had a natural talent for using swords and knives. The kid could also shoot an arrow with incredible accuracy. It was mind-blowing.

"Come and sit down," Fenris said as he put his arm around my shoulder. I leaned over and kissed Fenris on the cheek before following him and Estesius to the table beside Connell and Granger. Craig and Raleigh sat opposite us and smiled as I sat down.

"I think we need to talk about what is going to happen now that you are mated to someone from the Wild Claw Pack," Craig said.

I nodded my head; it had been something that had been on my mind. Technically I was still the head alpha of the Palecrest Pack but mated to the head alpha of Wild Claw meant that we were in two different worlds.

"I would like to stay here," I responded. "If that is okay with Fenris and Estesius."

"I will follow you wherever you go," Estesius answered.

Craig smiled and nodded. "That's what I thought you would say. But I've been thinking and talking with Petra. How about we bring Palecrest here. This war will not happen overnight, and Petra worries about the pack being without one of us."

"Did she like the idea of coming here?" I asked.

Craig grinned and nodded his head. "Yeah. Many of the pack had been asking why they couldn't come to Lalbert too."

My eyes widened, and my mouth dropped open. "Seriously?"

Craig chuckled. "Yeah. We have missed brother. And they all know that you have found your mate and are expecting a baby. Plus, they want to meet Brandon and Langley."

"Well, I guess that answers that, then. You think we could find land here somewhere?" I asked Connell, who was sitting beside me.

Connell nodded his head. "Yeah. I actually know that the land to the south of us, across the creek, is for sale."

"Shit, really?" I gasped.

Connell chuckled and nodded his head. "Yep. Almost like it was just meant to be, huh?"

"Yeah. That's weird," I responded before looking over at Craig. "It will take a little while to build housing there."

"That's not necessarily true," Anghus said from his position further down the table. "I don't like manipulating my children's powers, but Canea can create worlds with her mind."

My mouth dropped open as I stared at the gargoyle with shock. "Are you serious?"

Anghus chuckled and nodded his head. "As a hole in the head."

"Well, I guess the Palecrest Pack is moving to Lalbert."

Craig grinned and reached out his knuckles to bump mine. Fenris slung his arm around my shoulders and kissed my cheek before doing the same to Estesius. I couldn't believe what was like a blink of an eye; we were getting prepared to settle into a new home. And I was a father to two children and about to have a third. I never suspected my life to turn out this way, but there wasn't going to be a day that went by that I wasn't thrilled with the outcome.

Epilogue

E stesius

    "That's it, Estesius. One more big push, and Aretha will be here," Diana said as I grit my teeth and bore down. Tears streamed down my cheeks. I'd never felt so overwhelmed and yet at peace in all my life.

Fenris lifted our daughter reverently and carefully placed her on my chest. Aretha fell into the waiting arms of Fenris with a shriek. I looked down at her and smiled as her blonde hair stuck to her head. Aretha opened her eyes, and the purple irises stared into my soul.

"Welcome to the world, little one," I whispered as I kissed her head.

My daughter. She was here, and I couldn't be happier. Once Craig and Boyd decided to move the Palecrest Pack over to Lalbert, everything seemed to move much faster. Canea had literally built houses with her mind. Like the Devil's Advocates, the houses were built into the trees. Anyone passing by would have assumed that they were looking into a forest.

The kids had been in awe watching Canea do her work. Apparently, Canea and Langley had been the ones that came up with the design. I loved it. Langley and Brandon were flourishing. From the angry little boy that first came to us to know a boy who laughed and was so easygoing. They'd made best friends and were doing fabulously in their classes.

We heard that Ettore was furious over Vex's death and planning retaliation, but none had been. We were all prepared, though. We still don't know what it was that they wanted me for. We could only assume that it was because I am a demi-god. They wanted my powers or maybe my body to produce children. I didn't know. Either way, I was glad I got out of there. I was so thankful to Arcadia, who risked her life for me. Someday I didn't feel like I deserved it.

"Congratulations, Estesius, Boyd, and Fenris," Diana said as Fenris cut the cord connecting Aretha to the placenta.

I looked over at my mates with a smile. "I love you both."

"We love you too," Boyd answered.

"I'll just get you cleaned up, and then we can bring the kids in if you like," Larissa suggested. "I know they are desperate to meet their little sister."

The kids had been so excited. The minute I went into labor, they told Boyd and Fenris that they had to get me to the medical unit. I chuckled. I could see the concern in Brandon's eyes and had to assure him that I would be fine and that all of this was normal.

Once I'd been cleaned up and wearing a pair of pajamas, I moved into a bed where I would stay the night with my family by my side. Boyd went out to fetch Brandon and Langley, and it didn't take long before the room was whole again.

"Come and meet your sister," I said with a smile.

Langley and Brandon came over to the bed with wide eyes. Langley climbed onto the bed beside me while Brandon stood on my other side.

"She's beautiful," Langley gushed.

"She sure is. What do you think, Brandon?" I asked.

The boy looked up at me with the most rugged look. "I'm going to protect her with my life. Just as I did with Langley."

I smiled and nodded my head. I reached out my hand and stroked it over his head. "I believe you. But unlike with Langley, you won't have the same pressure on you. Here you are free to be a kid and enjoy having two little sisters to love and teach."

Brandon smiled, and tears welled in his eyes. "Estesius?"

"Yes, love?"

"Can I call you Mama?"

Tears burned in my eyes, and I felt like a lump in my throat. "Of course," I sobbed as I pulled Brandon into my arms. I'd never felt so much love explode from my heart as I did that minute.

When I pulled back, Brandon looked up at Boyd and Fenris, who was crying just as hard as I was. "And I can call you Papa and Dad."

My mates nodded, and a sob fell from Fenris's lips. "I'd be honored."

"As would I," Boyd answered.

"Mama, Papa, and Dad," Boyd smiled.

The best thing that had ever happened to me was the beginning of this war. I couldn't believe how lucky my life had gotten, not only in finding our mate but also in having a baby and being blessed with Brandon and Langley.

When I got home the following day, the Palecrest Pack was waiting for us and cheering as we climbed out of the car. That afternoon was a sea of visitors. Everyone had brought meals and gifts for the kids and wanted to cuddle Aretha. She was such a peaceful little girl and happily went to anyone that wanted to hold her.

That night as we sat in the living room watching television, the door swung open, and Craig came bustling into the house.

"Sorry guys, I know you just got home, but another attack has occurred."

"Shit," Boyd said as he stood. "What is it?"

"Ettore, we think, has attacked the Onyx Rebels headquarters again."

I'd known that the Onyx Rebels had to move out to Louis Santos's childhood home because their original headquarters had been burned down.

"The Santos home?" Fenris clarified.

"Yep. There are several deaths."

"Shit," Boyd swore again. "What do they need?"

"Kade is holding a meeting at the Devil's Advocates compound."

Boyd and Fenris nodded their heads and stood. "You stay here, baby; I will ring you and put you on speaker so you can hear what is being said," Boyd said.

I smiled and nodded my head. "Be safe."

Boyd leaned down and kissed my lips. "Always, baby. Always."

One of the things we had done when we bought the Palecrest pack was form tunnels beneath the land that led from the Devil's Advocates to the Wild Claw pack lands to here. This way, no one had to leave the warded areas, which meant we were safe. It gave me assurance for my family and made it easier for us to get between places.

"Do you think Ettore will try to attack here?" Brandon asked, pulling my attention to him.

I hummed. "I don't know. I don't know that he will necessarily be able to. This place is warded pretty heavily. But then I'd assumed that the Onyx Rebels were too."

"When they came here, and we talked to Hildr, she said they got some new members. I wonder if they were double agents."

"With Ettore, anything is possible. We will have to wait to see what the next installment in this damned war brings." I hummed.

"Yeah. Hopefully, his death."

I nodded my head. It was my hope too.

The end.

Don't miss out!

Visit the website below and you can sign up to receive emails whenever S L Davies publishes a new book. There's no charge and no obligation.

https://books2read.com/r/B-A-NZRR-MYREC

BOOKS 2 READ

Connecting independent readers to independent writers.

Did you love *Fenris*? Then you should read *Rising Sun*[1] by S L Davies!

[2]

Humans have shared Earth with Supernatural beings since the beginning of time. They co-inhabited peacefully for the most part. Supernatural's stayed hidden, and Human's went about life blissfully unaware.All of that was going to change! God had been missing for thousands of years. Angel convinced humans and Supernatural alike that the message of hate they spread came directly from God. They convinced everyone that Lucifer was the evil entity when in fact, it was the Angels filled with hatred, jealousy, and greed.When the Angels make the plan to take over the Earth realm and enslave humans and Supernatural alike, war is threatened.Hunter was a girl who grew up abused, broken, and torn down. She prayed that God would protect her or just kill her. It took twenty-three years before she got her to wish. Gunned down on the

1. https://books2read.com/u/m2dEvk

2. https://books2read.com/u/m2dEvk

street, she finds herself in Hell, with a new job as a Succubus Demon, allowing her to wreak revenge on those that wronged her. During this reaping, she meets Heath the Necromancer, Jagger the Witch, Kynan the Nephilim, and Jye the Jinn. They are the hottest guys she has ever seen, and they all want her. She wants them and Lucifer. With their unconventional relationship, they form a bond and team. Together they will help bring the Angels to justice and protect the Earth realm from the threat of violence. **This is a stand-alone Reverse Harem. The steam level is high. There are triggering subjects. Suitable to 18+ M/M scenes included.**

Read more at https://www.amazon.com/~/e/B0832T8F7Z.

Also by S L Davies

Breeding Facility
Memphis
Bacchus
Coltrane
Pax
Raiden
Nash
Breeding Facility

Devil's Advocates
Lynx
Israel
Jai
Jasper
Arley
Zion
Oakland

KINK
Gunner

Newlyn
Aina
Ione
Freya
Tanquil

Obsidian Mechanics
Donte
Atticus
Boden
Stagger

Onyx Rebels
Onyx Rebels Prologue
Hawke
Rison
Bandit
Butler
Nova

Rigby Brothers
Asher
Burgess
Macklin
Drake
Jericho
Obsidian

Second Chances
Bunny
Caged
By The Sword
The Cult
Rising Sun
Forbidden Bound
Christmas Escape
Executioner
Maid for the Doms

Watch for more at https://www.amazon.com/~/e/B0832T8F7Z.

About the Author

S L Davies is an Australian Author living in Country, Victoria. She is inspired by the world around her.

Read more at https://www.amazon.com/~/e/B0832T8F7Z.